This Little Tiger book belongs to:

_____

_____

_____

To the little lords and ladies of Lumby –
Andrew, Daisy, Elizabeth, Grace,
Jack, Jennifer, Kate, Laura,
Samantha and Sophie
~ H R

For Venus, Matthew
and baby Esme x
~ M S

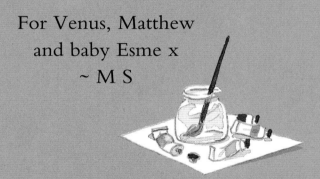

LITTLE TIGER PRESS LTD,
an imprint of the Little Tiger Group
1 Coda Studios, 189 Munster Road, London SW6 6AW
www.littletiger.co.uk

First published in Great Britain 2002
This edition published 2020

Printed in China • LTP/1800/3385/0820

2 4 6 8 10 9 7 5 3 1

The Princess's Secret Letters

Hilary Robinson   Mandy Stanley

LiTTLE TiGER

LONDON

Last year I sent Princess Isabella a birthday card.

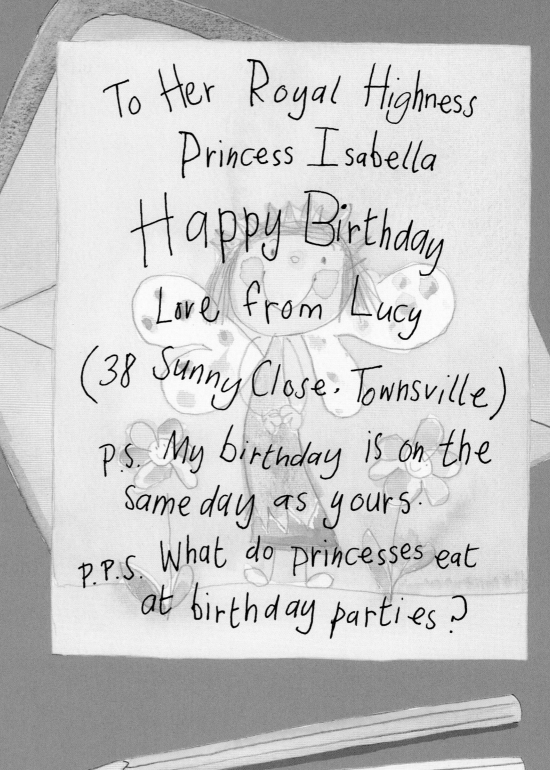

To Her Royal Highness
Princess Isabella
Happy Birthday
Love from Lucy
(38 Sunny Close, Townsville)
P.S. My birthday is on the same day as yours.
P.P.S. What do princesses eat at birthday parties?

Dear Lucy,

Her Royal Highness Princess Isabella has asked me to write and thank you for your card. She is thrilled to learn that you share the same birthday.

Her Royal Highness has also asked me to say that, officially, the birthday menu includes cucumber sandwiches (no crusts), fruit cake and scones.

But secretly, the
Princess eats . . .

. . . *pizza!*

38 Sunny Close, Townsville.

Dear Princess Isabella,

Thank you for your letter. I like pizzas too! Can you tell me, do you have an entertainer at your party? I have TRICKY TREVOR - the magic man at mine. He makes gigantic monkeys from balloons.

Love Lucy

Yum